Paperback edition 2022
Cover design: Bethany McKay ©
ISBN: 9780646858050

EBook edition 2022
ISBN: 9780646858067

Published by Creative Inktuition
www.creativeinktuition.com

***

I wish to acknowledge the Wurundjeri of the Kulin Nation on which this book was printed and written. I pay my respects to Indigenous Elders past, present and emerging.
It always was and always will be, Aboriginal land.

SINK
OR
SWIM

Written by Dominik Shields
Illustrated by Bethany McKay

For my dearest Jesse & Beth.

There is a sea inside of you,
it rages louder than you could handle.
After all this time it still wasn't able to pass through,
you thought you had broken,
but my darling,
look how you grew.

FINE LINE

Walking between like and lust
now wanting to see you in daylight, not only at dusk.

It is a delicate thing
to walk the line between friend or fling,
to kiss you in the dark and then to be kept apart,
to have you on my mind and in my heart
keeping it cool is a delicate art.

Electricity runs between us at night
our bodies tucked into each other,
I'm resisting the urge to fight or flight.
I didn't think I'd have space in my chest for another.

Folk songs play in the dark
rain pouring it's feelings to the soft earth below -
I did not think flowers could bloom, when a garden wasn't ready
to sow.

May tastes sweeter because of you,
with your lips on my neck,
I hope you're still here in June.

THE LOVE YOU LONG FOR

Today I saw an elderly man ask a stranger for help so he could
video call his wife,
to show her the ducks he had found

'Because she has loved them all her life'

.

Being with you is like looking in a mirror
except now instead of imperfections,
I've found a gentle understanding
that wasn't there before.

You told me I was beautiful,
and said it in a way that finally made me believe it.

WAKING IS MUCH SWEETER

I stopped dreaming the day I met you,
nights once filled with vivid memories and wanted distractions,
are now blissful dark spaces.
Time passes quickly knowing
I'll be seeing you in the morning.

Stolen kisses next to a pool table at midnight,
I'd happily lose a game every time.

Morning light looks different from your side of the room.
The way it dances from behind your blinds, a private moment
reserved for just us two.

You curl around my body just as your ivy does your desk, you
mumble in my ear about needing coffee,
but instead you hold me a little tighter and fall back into rest.

Things are moving slowly, a welcomed change of pace,
it amazes me still,
that I get to wake up next to you, my nose pressed against your
face.

I'm stuck between running away and
the nook in your neck.

PINK MOON, PINK LIGHT

When your eyes locked onto mine by the light of your lamp,
you shook hair from your eyes, my breath shook out of my body,
grazing my cheek with your stubble,
Oh mercy, help me now,
for I'm in a lot of trouble.

PINK MOON, PINK LIGHT

From the minute you said hello
I had no idea what I was going to do,
you smiled, I came undone -
this is the feeling of a new someone.

HONEYBEE

Darling honeybee
how ever do you stay so busy
with eyes that weigh so heavy?
From one hive to the other
you flicker, here, there,
yet when the day is done you still have time to sing
your sweet melodies to me.

When the moon is right,
take to your pen and your paper,
speak your incantations to the dark, then set them alight.
Everything that you long for, will come true,
if there is enough belief within you.

The feeling of your skin against mine on winter mornings,
is like the sun as you emerge from the freezing sea.

NOT PRETTY ENOUGH TO HANG IN THE GALLERY

For years I squeezed and shrunk myself into the tiniest frame possible,
yet you still did not hang me on your wall.

You love and then you leave.

What else did I expect
from the boy
with eyes as clouded as the green
sea?

The conversation flows easily
from dawn to dark.
Softly
softly
open up a piece of my fractured heart.

Scent of burning pine
the ice of winter forming on the tip of my nose.
You draped around me like my favourite cardigan
I never thought I'd ever be able to thaw my heart out,
and feel like this again.

Your teeth chattered
my arms wrapped around your body
'My brain isn't usually this scattered' your voice a whisper.
Our breath guided us as we walked in silence
noses frosty, fingers blue
my eyes sneaking glances at you.

LOCKED DOWN,
AGAIN

25 kilometers has never felt so far away

until now.

STARGAZING AT YOU

Now I know how astronomers feel when they discover a new
star.
How their world lights up a little brighter,
their nights are no longer a lingering look in the dark.

April was an unexpected adventure, we stumbled through May.

You kept me laughing throughout June and I felt my walls come down as the sun circled around the new moon.

I find solace in the sheets of someone new,
of you.
Your denim jacket, the sounds on your street
& the dogs in your bed.

My heart cannot take seeing you again
for I do not trust that it won't destroy
the life that I have finally started to build
without
You.

GRACE

Your face
your waist
an air of grace
you wrap me in a long embrace
I think this is where I will misplace
the thoughts of them that once took up space.

I pushed you away in an attempt for us to heal
for us to grow into who we are meant to be.
You returned into my life in the Spring,
like the ivy that covers the walls of the houses we used to look
at.

I thought I'd be able to prune the vines away,
so my walls didn't crumble under the weight of your love,
what a fool I was to think
you would ever leave.

Your name rolls off my tongue
as easily as you fell into my life.

The darkest nights have been playing on my mind,
longing to have another by my side.
Easing the thoughts in my head,
hoping that they will silence the noise inside.

I do not wish to wake you, disturb your peace, make you want to retreat.

I keep my voice quiet, trying to tame the demons that rest in my throat.

Yet, you take the darkest parts of my mind and light them up with everything that you are.

Blowing off all the plans I had
to be curled in your lap
your head balanced upon my shoulder blades, arms either
side of my waist,
a small sacrifice to make.

BITTERSWEET

There's a bitterness when you say my name.
In the way you would say that you're fine.
Dismiss me. Dismiss us.
Make me feel as if I wasn't enough.
I waited for you to make up your mind, waited for you to
take your time.
I cried, you sighed, you left, I wept.
The sweetener of you leaving, the only thing that cuts
through my salt,
I remember that we will heal in time.

One day we will be just fine.

You curse my name for truths that you did not want to hear and you're haunted by the apparitions you created on your own.
Casting your projections onto me, your guilt merely passing through these eyes of mine.
You were the one to place the nail in the coffin, the one to show me who you really are,
the disillusions in your mind being the one to end us this time.

I did not think I could falter
under the weight of your gaze,
that was before I had not seen you in days.

The ghost that haunts me is now silenced when you speak my name, they are put to bed when you lay beside me.

The ghost in my head lays in a box underneath my bed while I am with you, the dreams that it wishes to steal are outweighed by new emotions I am able to feel.

The ghost in my head will be buried and long forgotten but shall not be dead.

You speak of empathy as if its a currency
something to barter with,
something that you need permission to possess
I hold the weight of the worlds sorrow in my hands
I carry the light of the worlds love in my chest.

We give weight to the words we speak
I will conjure your name
let it be the curse that hangs upon my lips
until they cannot handle the strength of it anymore.

You held my hand in public
& that was enough.

Soak in the bath half the day, emptying my mind.
Washing myself of you, your cologne and the feeling that
you left behind.
That is, until I can bathe in you again and sink under your
weight.

HEY, GIRLIE

Hey girlie,
with your big brown eyes looking into mine
your jacket pulled around your ears
I hear you down the hallway, your heels clicking three
times, making your way back to me.
The way you grumble in your sleep
softly is how you speak
the sweet secrets that you keep, mumbled only to me.
Hey girlie
hey girlie where you been?
hey girlie come on back to me,
I hope there are no terrors waiting for you when you dream
hey girlie come back to me,
hey girlie make your way back to me.

Home was wherever I was without him.
Closed off to everyone else that tried to break down walls,
unable to fully open the door.

I realised it was holding space inside of a different person.
It was me all along,
I held the key to my own home and didn't know until I was
left all alone.

I haven't been sleeping any better,
than when your hand was under my sweater.
I haven't slept for days,
waiting for you to come and help me escape.

What am I to do,
when my mind is so preoccupied
with you?

THANK GOD FOR GOODBYES

You made me miserable
& my body knew before my heart had the guts to tell you.

The tree that saw us break up, was hit by lightning.

Now, it blooms.

Funny how everything worked out, by saying goodbye to you.

Am I just the jacket to keep you warm until you make your way out of winter and back into the arms of a summer lover?

IT'S NOT HAYFEVER, I'M CRYING AGAIN

Watching the way the wattle grew
reminds me how out of the blue
my eyes and nose would run
just the same
every time I thought of you.

You,
just like a firecracker, you brought the colour I was lacking,
green, purple and orange, flashes in my eyes.

It started out with a bang.

Bright colours and sound burst into my life and then just as
quickly as you arrived,

this fizzled out into nothing.

The thoughts in your head weigh you down
so take refuge in my bed and see if it will help drown them
out.

STARVING FOR LOVE

Living off the crumbs of your affections
waiting for a lover,
who's eyes still belong to another.

METAMORPHOSIS

Butterflies have flown towards the Spring
leaving their broken cocoons
where my lungs used to be.

HATE TO MISS YOU

I pretend not to need you,
wearing a mask upon my face, hoping that it will make
true,
but, I've never been a good liar.

Avoiding the places that I can't walk through,
places I dare to tread
in case I see your head.

The wolves at my door wait silently for me to crumble,
for my skin to open old wounds, to be consumed once
again by you.
They do not snarl, they do not bite, they wish to keep their
appetite,
holding out for the day that I open the door and slink
towards me like I am the cure.

Weather will not deter them, curses will not disarm them.
I am stuck with wolves at my door,
paralysed upon the floor,
I can lead the pack but only when I have enough strength
to be able to fight back.

SPRING FLING

Maybe a crush is all this is meant to be
for I do not think my body
could take someone else ripping
the romance out of me.

Tell me whose lips I've been kissing
because they don't seem to match
the soul or face
of the man I've been missing.

L.A WEATHER

A boy in California set my heart on fire,
he looked at me, the sunset in his eyes, with salt water hair.
Pointing towards the ocean he told me not to worry about
the horizon,
there was always something good on the other side,

*"You have to hold on, until you find it, even on the days it
gets too hard to try."*

A boy from California held onto my heart, until it was
strong enough to live inside my chest on its own.

NUMBER ONE

Today I saw a woman tell her partner she was going to
have a baby,
he looked at her as if he had just found God.

Gazing upon this woman as if he stumbled upon the
meaning of life,
I have never seen a man beam brighter than the sun
until she told him he was the only person
she could envision holding their new number one.

LAZY LOVE

There is one love that is purer than the rest
it is the one you carry deep within your chest,
you feel it often,
who it comes from is up to you
they are your souls person to choose.

It may be your mother, lover, sibling, your best friend
or perhaps it has four paws and a tail at its end.

It comes unannounced and humble
it shows you who you are when you crumble,
it builds you up and it keeps you sane
it is a lazy love
but the truest love all the same.

FLIGHT

The man with the aviary feeds his birds in the shade,
I watch him surrender to these creatures every single day.
His eyes light up as he kisses them good morning,
his voice so high as he sings to them so sweetly,
what it must be like to hold so much love for something
other than yourself
other than a lover.

I watch as the birds nestle in his neck, their wings softly
tap against his face
they know him and how he has created a safe space.

It brings a tear to my eye
I see these beautiful, tiny things hold so much love for a
man
who keeps them locked away in a metal cage.

Cherry blossoms help me reminisce
of the way the sun would kiss
my cheeks when I was 8.
A time before I knew how my life would complicate,
by growing up, growing in and growing out of the things
that once made sense.

Would you stay
if I left my heart locked up
in a cage
so that nothing between us would change?

Love is just a word
waking up next to you on a Tuesday morning
was the feeling.

You asked me what I wanted
& my soul said:
the feeling of the autumn sun on my belly,
my cheeks burning like ripened peaches,
for the stars to align,
to taste sweet delights without guilt,
to feel salt against my skin from the Italian sea,

Yet all that came out of my mouth was:
Nothing, really.

You touched the darkest parts of my skin
with golden hands
an alchemy I don't pretend to understand.

Steal a kiss in the dark
break my heart
again.
It was to grow cold after you'd gone
leaving me to open my chest,
to repair it in the morning sun.

I curse my eyes
for letting me fall under the guise
of another lovers demise
waiting until the turning of the tides
where I won't be left holding my tortured pride.

Nothing is permanent
except for us saying goodbye this time.

India, Russia and Rome
places meant to visit as a two,
I will keep our plans in the depths of my chest
safely in tow
so I can tell you about them
once I've seen them on my own.

My mind lingers on thoughts of you
while my body reminds me to let it go.
The way that you would make me feel
still cuts me down to the bone.
I don't want to get over you, but I have to, otherwise I'll
drown.

All my dreams of running into you,
now terrors in the night
on the off chance that I do.
My heart splits in two
whenever I think of you,
I remember the warmth of your smile,
how you'd always make me feel safe,
even if you had to hold me a little longer each once in a
while.

How you would cup my face and that would be the safest
space for us to remain.

Then you changed.
I haven't experienced a pain like this before.

As if I had lost the one who made it all make sense.

Now just a ghost that I hide beneath my bed.
The one you used to be now locked away in the depths of
my head,
submerged,
by the creature that took over.

Remember when I sewed the hole in your jeans
while you still had them on?
You asked me not to stab you with the needle
I told you I'd never hurt you on purpose
(I never lied)
When the stitches broke and the hole reopened
I said sorry, embarrassed I couldn't fix it,
you said not to worry because our love was stronger than
any gaping hole
(You lied)

BLACK OR BLUE

Boys in white cars
will promise you the moon and the stars,
paint your nights black
with fabricated tales of *'you'll never feel blue'*
until they decide that they've had enough
and break your little heart in two.

I confess I'm bereft
for the romanticised version of you
that I know will never be able to hold on to.
You hold space in my head, cradle it with hands worn
unknowingly ripping apart the seams
that should not have been torn.
Longing to go back to a place that I can never return to
for I am not me and you are not you
we grew, both up and apart
and I think that's the worst thing about it.

I want to feel the same butterflies in my stomach, as I did
in Greece.
Waking up to notes from you, on the other side of the
world,
how your day had turned into night, how you were hoping
to see me soon.

Forever chasing the feeling, the sun upon the horizon,
take me back to the Mediterranean, where the hardest part
of my day
was to lie on the beach or read in the shade.

Waiting for the day I could fall asleep next to your winter
skin, worlds away,
there were Greecian cats scratching outside my door
and only a few more weeks until I could come home to
you.

BASOREXIA:
an overwhelming desire to kiss

It begins as a faint feeling, like trying to remember a
distant memory.
What was it I needed?
Who was it I wanted?
As the days turn into weeks it grows louder, tapping upon
your rib cage:
Titter tatter, we still matter.
It sneaks it's way into your dreamscape, asking a little
louder if you will please pay attention,
only when you wake, it screams. Deafening.
Like cymbals in your ears.
The marching band is getting closer.
Will our lips touch now, or will it be later?
Don't leave me lonely for too long,
or I'll forget how our symphonies used to converge into
one song,
it sustains me when I feel I cannot go on.

HE SMELLED LIKE CITRUS
TASTED LIKE THE SEA

I hope that you can catch the dream
that you have been chasing,
I hope that it makes you happy
as you deserve that feeling.

When I write about you it makes me sound sappy.

I suppose that's what a true love does,
turns your world upside down and inside out,
reminds you that there's goodness around.
You made me smile, you made me cry,
& you helped me feel alive.

LACUNA:
a blank space

Sometimes I think it would be better to feel nothing at all
to sit and watch the world pass idly by
to feel myself completely void and emotions run dry
how simple it must be to have a blank space where your
heart should be
to live in the comfort of nothing.

SHORT LIVED ROMANCES
WITH EVERY BARISTA
IN MELBOURNE

My glasses fog, my cheeks blush,
our hands touch.
'How was your day? Did you want a pastry? It's on me."
It would be rude to say no.

I stutter out a thank you, the black coffee spilling from the
cup and down my sleeve
I walk hastily back onto the street.
Light laughter follows me as I go,
I can't come back here tomorrow.

The fire in my chest, caused me months of unrest
because you couldn't figure out what you wanted to do.

How could I just be a placeholder for you?

You told me I meant more to you than you could express,
yet I was the one left crying in detest
of your indecision.

You grew up so beautiful.

Yet you did not realise that it was not the outside, people
saw,
they did not gravitate towards the architecture of your face,
how your eyes catch the light, the way your mouth curves
at the edges when you smile,
or the fact that your hair falls perfectly into place.

Your soul is brighter than you will ever know,
how lucky we are to feel it's glow.

A day well spent, underneath your covers until the darkness steals the light.
A shelter from the storm that continues to rage, a constant place to hide.
If the world is falling apart, I wouldn't mind, as long as I had you to sit beside.

Sometimes I wonder why I was given the gift to read
and eventually the gift to write
when I am so disheartened by those who spin words much
more eloquently than I.

The breath from your lungs
does more for my skin
than the wind ever does.

Off to a good start, sweetheart,
what a shame it is to be kept far apart
from the one that makes you forget
the noise inside of your head
and not just when you're in their bed.

Throw what you know to the wall
they are just cowards who only seem to answer the call
of what aids them at the time, what serves them when it
feels right.
It is not your burden to carry
for your mark on the world is greater than that
of those with a shallow mind.

Their arrows merely flashes
upon the landscape of your life.

Do not sacrifice yourself for those that will only toss you
aside
when they have taken what they want and no longer wish
to abide.

Big eyed boys with sandalwood skin
letting me think that we were akin
in our ideology, our minds aligned.
Silly me,
once again being led in the wrong direction,
my mind too expansive for you to travel, my heart bigger
than my body.

SINK OR SWIM

The most dangerous thing is to love
to feel the weight of it
to sink without a way to raise your head above
water.

How fortunate we are to receive this dreaded gift from
above
when our ships hit the waves that cascade
it lingers in our lungs
fires from our fingertips
like scavengers on a raid.

How unfortunate it is, to love and feel its sting in return.

I've missed you, honey
like wrens miss the sunrise in winter,
or the moon does the sun, with the passing of time.
You have bewitched a part of me that I did not think could
feel lightness again.

Frozen for the bulk of my days
kept inside like a bird in a cage, unable to feel the strength
of the sun upon my face.
I feel like I am living in a state of paralysis,
unable to break out of a chrysalis,
condemned to live inside of a prison built
upon the mouths of demons, covered in silt.
Their eyes gleam, their hands hook to my sides,
they know I won't be able to outrun them this time.

You tread where I cannot follow,
towards a place that is unknown, a place reserved just for you.
A journey that is meant to be experienced without the shadow of your past
lingering in the dark, branding you with a mark
that you cannot shake.

You did not break, you bloomed.

I hope you have the same mercy as I did for you,
to let me finally flourish too.

Nothing but memories to you now,
I hope, at least, I'm a good one.

I loved you then and I love you still
time may pass and years will grow.

My piece of fool's gold
to always have and to hold.

I hear the colour blue when I see you,
you laughed and told me you hear it too.

I saw the way she broke your heart,
how your eyes lost their shine, cast down at your shoes
I knew then, I could never have you look at me like that.
You poured yourself out to me, I listened,
hoping that I would not be the next one you christened
with the power to make you feel the same way.

I'll hold you while your coffee cools and your skin warms
against mine.
Till your eyes give back into sleep
resting the bones that grow heavy, the weight of
expectation like a winter coat,
all around you the scent of sandalwood and pine,
today is not the day we ask *'will you be mine?'*
I'm happy to shoulder the burden until you change your
mind.

I miss the lips of those I should not long to kiss
as the weather turns sour and time passes away yet another
idle hour.
I sit and wonder how I came to be this way
what part of you still resides in me, that seeks out the
comfort of something that couldn't stay.

Always had a heart for seeking out for something new
yet in the depths of my soul I knew only one thing true -

I would never be magnificent enough for you.

I endeavour to keep myself together
I poured myself into you, hoping my love would sink
through
to make you see how I cared for you.
It's a shame I can't go to
parts of this city,
because you were the one that made them glow,
all I feel now is unease and shitty.

You,
hellbent on making sure my love has been spent
on nobody else but you.

Did you think it would end this way?
Or did you think I'd break so easily that I'd just stay?

I hope that you can find
the ease of a quietened mind
to give you the peace and rest that you seek
restlessness will not last forever
as the days are no longer grey
you too will begin to feel better.

MUSE

A shining light, a guiding genius,
one that renders you speechless.
They left you dreamless, your mind consumed with their
skin perfumed,
you ache, they take, you give and their magic will outlive.
Do not give in
to soft eyes or a wide grin
to those who give their affections out on a whim.
You have been misused
by the one you named your muse,
does having something beautiful to look at,
make the anguish worth it?

Try to keep intrusive thoughts from creeping into your head,
when under the covers of a lover who wishes you were someone else instead.

I watched as a boy broke his partners heart in two
there they both sat under a sky of clear blue.
A subtle tear fell from her eye as he explained to her why
they could not be together
she blinked them free
got up to leave
and did not stop to say goodbye.

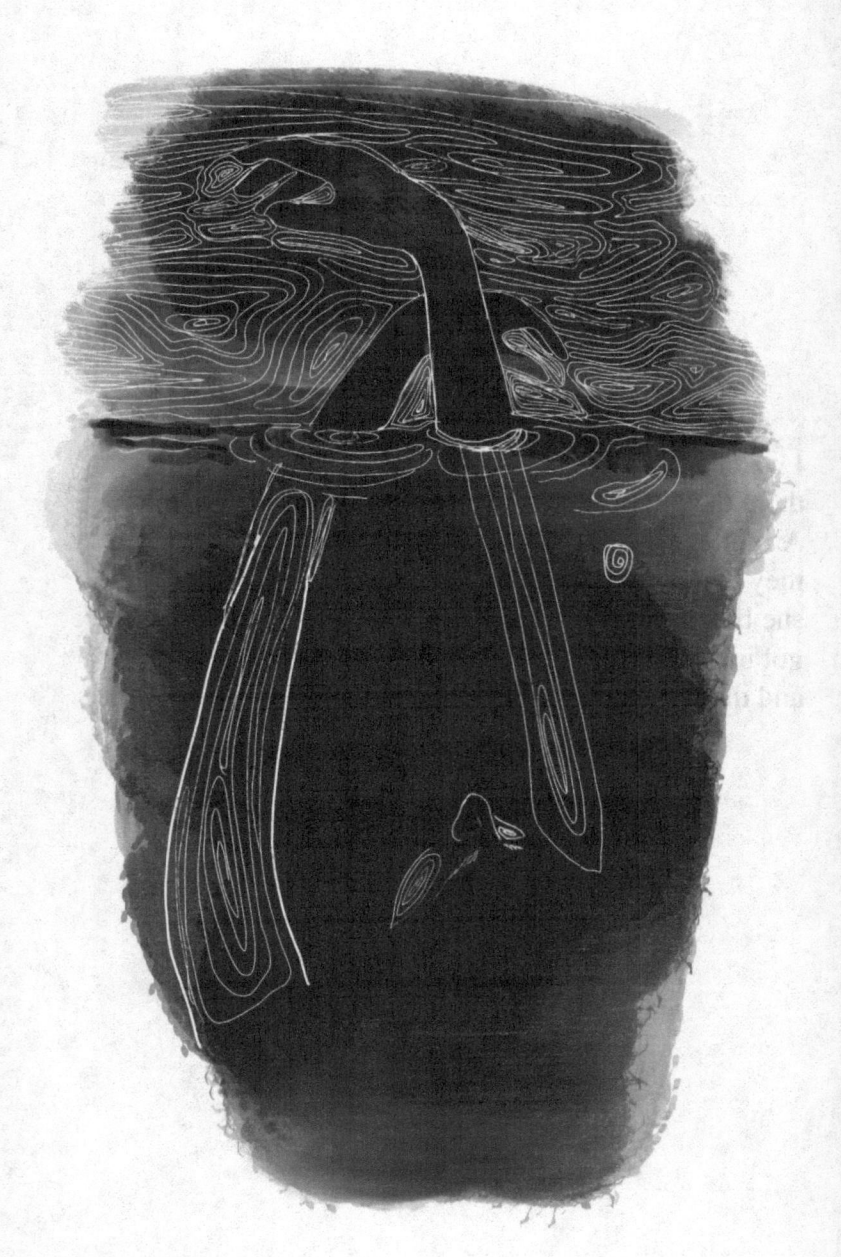

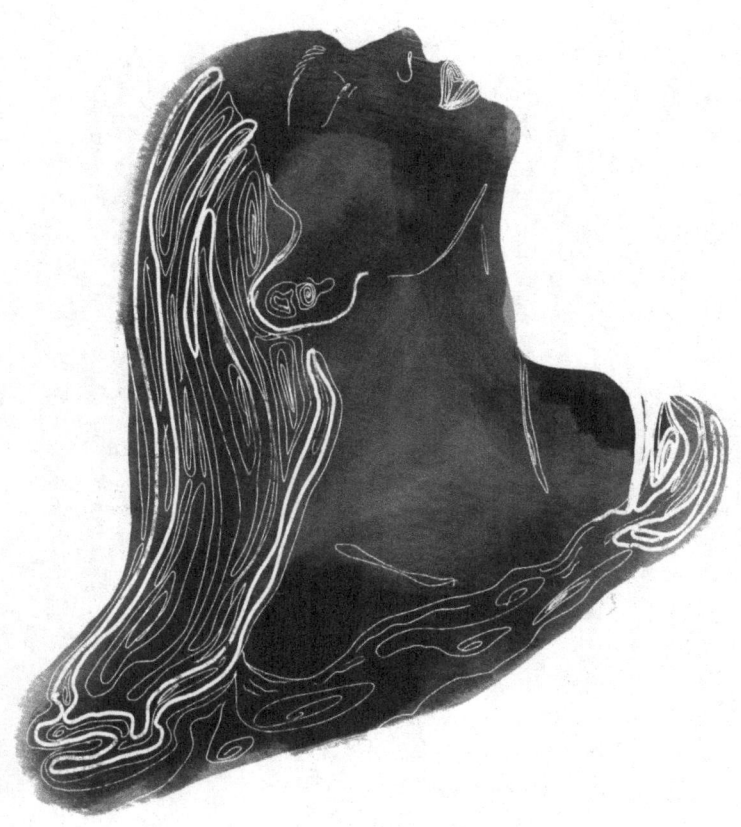

Happy birthday,
a text I'll never send, because it will hurt us both if I do.
I have a lot of wishes for you, my hope is they come true.
I have re-written this letter more times than you will know,
my hands are ink stained blue.
I hope that this year, your next phase of life, is as electric
as you have grown to be.
That you smile wider than you have in the past year, that
you push through fear, that your mind and heart work
together to be kinder to you.

I hope your scales balance on both sides and your air
remains calm.
Keep your head in the clouds, sunlight has always looked
better on you.

This year you will find out what pieces were missing and
they will come together like a jigsaw we could never finish.
Notice how brilliant you are, even on the days you don't
think so.

I wish for us to share another laugh, eyes crinkled at the
edges, stomachs aching, mouths wide. Another hug, warm
and safe.
I wish for you to celebrate exactly who you are at this
moment.

Happy birthday for now and until the day I can tell you
again in person.

I FELL IN LOVE WITH A LAKE NAMED JENNY

I'd never seen something so pure before,
I fell in love with the way she looked that day;

The glimmer of her surfaces, how the sun would expose
the secrets kept in her shade.
The air was sweet, it smelled like pine and fresh rain.
The earth was warm, the colour of fresh caramel. It
bewitched me, completely.
Pebbles sat in her waters, fallen siblings of the mountain
range that held her close.
Kept safe underneath snow capped rock, it hung like a fur
coat,
she stayed sheltered from winter kisses.

I longed to feel safe, to feel like I was home,
for a place for my roots to grow, endless and expansive,
somewhere that would let me roam.

When I looked at her I felt it, I had found what I was
looking for,
from the moment my grey eyes turned to her blue waters.
I was never going to feel like this again,
pines held me close, the mountains kept me safe and she
gave my heart a reason to try one more time.

I LEFT MY HEART IN UTAH BUT FOUND MY SOUL IN ARIZONA

The morning was cold, beads of frost upon my nose,
wrapped in three blankets,
I could not bring myself to leave the cocoon I'd made.
There would be no metamorphosis today.

Another year around the sun, another year of
responsibilities, of anxieties, not even the covers could
stave these away.

5am had shouted my name, my body aching in reply, my
mind consumed with thoughts of if, when and why.
The sun had not risen yet, a calmness shrouded you and
I, our feet crunching leaves outside the only sound to be
heard.

There is beauty in morning stillness, in the sound of the
cuckoo and the wind as it passes through pine branches.

Eyes adjusting to darkness, breath flowing like a cigarette,
steaming black coffee bringing life back to the tips of my
fingers.

It was then, when I saw them, my world stopped.

My heart ceased to beat, my breath left my body.

There is something about a land untouched by human
hands,
an untamed beauty, raw and misshapen, like the haircuts of
the girls back home.

"The mountains wake up, one peak at a time here" an
elderly hiker told me, eyes clouded by tears.

Golden beams swept across cliff faces, tangerine and
terracotta chasms danced under the morning light.
The Colorado River snakes its way through the Canyon,
hugging the rock faces as it rushes towards Mexico.
Untouchable, vast and quick, it longs for a warmer lover,
leaving the Rocky Mountains behind.

I will never see beauty like this again; titans carved out of
rock, their strength unwavering through seasons, majesty in
its purest form.

I finally realised what being human felt like, staring at the
Canyon in front of me.

Never ending and forever changing.

I poured my heart out upon cream pages
you told me that you read them
my breath broke in my lungs and I wept until my bones
shook.
Part of me died
& the other part of me realised I was thankful that you
cared.

You read the words I lovingly wrote for you, spun them
into something that made sense in your head & then spat
them back towards me.

WHY DO YOU LIKE ME?

You remember the little things others don't think important.

Wide-eyed and sweet toothed
it's a shame you didn't have a taste for salt
for my tear coated skin holds enough for us both.

You thought I wasn't paying attention
that I didn't care, hiding in my books, behind my hair,
as words of a song I knew fell from your lips,
while a guitar rested on your hips.

The truth of it was
I was so overwhelmed by you
to keep my gaze for too long
would have given it away -
what I felt for you, were feelings starting to bloom.

TWENTY SIX

At twenty-six
I learnt there were places, people and situations I could not
fix
I held out my hands to the world
watched as I dropped the pearl back into the ocean of life
where it belonged.

I grew up and apart,
I listened to my soul and finally forgave my heart.
Horrors followed me everywhere I went
I did not think there would be a peaceful moment spent
I tried to drown them out, found myself sickened with
doubt.
I retreated inwards, silent and small.

Loving hands reached inside of my chest, pulling me back
to the light,
laughter overtook the pains in my heart,
I learnt to let go and I decided that I was the one who had
to finally let myself grow.

He taught his friend how to make sourdough
brown eyes watched him with a childlike intensity,
I have never seen two men speak so passionately
about the activity that kept them together
while the world was falling apart.

Counting down the days until my head is back in your lap
your hands in my hair & voice humming in my ears.
Counting down the days
until I don't have to count them anymore.

I'm living in the ashes of cigarettes that burned out long ago.

I still see your silhouette at the end of my bed
your rational voice inside of my head
telling me everything we did right
how neither of us gave it up without a fight
how you loved me then
and would until the very end -
If you can't be my lover
I'm content with being your friend
I'd rather have a little bit of you to hold
than to walk the rest of this earth alone.

It makes me beam
to witness how happy you seem
I hope that it's true,
for it is something I could not give you
at least at this point on our journey
I look forward to how far you travel
your new companion on your level.

I sit and wonder
if you ever ponder
on how we ended up in this space -
Me, crying each time I see your face
You, hoping you could reclaim your place.

The days now unknown
for we have outgrown
the cocoon we once shared
it was better to love and have dared
than not tried at all.

I hide my tears
sedate my fears.
For being awake
is just as cruel as when I let the night take
me back to the places I do not wish to go.

DIGITAL DAYS

Small screen,
I only see what you want me to
a memory
of a life I will never know, again
versions of you that I cannot experience.
Mentions of your name
make me delirious
I thought I'd be past all this
but
I cannot give up the way
the knife continues to twist.

DAILY AFFIRMATION

The scent of burning pine
a backdrop of a grey clouded sky
I've never felt more alive
than with the rain on my face
feet pressed to the ground

Inhale.

Look around.

It is your body's job to survive
it is up to your mind to help it thrive.
Do the things that make you come alive,
you cannot live in your shell forever
trust me, it can get better.

AN ODE TO MY DOG

There is a love that cannot be explained
by one who does not even know your name.
Your new favourite place seems to be snoring loudly next
to my face,
'No dogs on the bed!' we'll just fabricate another story
instead.

Every morning you greet me with a grunt and a wiggle,
I see how you grow, you take up the space that was
designed just for you,
I would not dare call you the litter runt, oh, how you shake
your butt makes me giggle.

You understand my mind in a way that I cannot,
you hold my heart in yours without a second thought.
I do not know what I did to deserve you,
my best friend and my saviour, I don't know how I will
ever repay the favour.

Big brown eyes that have only ever known kindness
You are strong and you are silent,
it is only when it reaches dinner time that you are no longer
quiet.

From now till the end of our days,
there will be that wide smile upon your face,
I will make sure that this is the place,
you feel at home and the most safe,
where you are loved and adored
until that last moment your golden paws touch the floor.

WOUNDS

Each day they close
as the months go by the hole seems smaller.
Then out of nowhere
there you are,
your eyes a reflection in mine
your smile against a pale blue sky.
A view in the afternoon
of *what could be, one day soon*.
Each day they open
as the weeks go by the hole seems bigger.

It wasn't what I thought it was
no if's or buts or because.
It was easy, it was fun
you never made my eyes run.

Soft and gentle
it was all in the mental
& now I'm trying to decipher
why I let myself linger
for way too long.

LESSONS IN GRIEF

Grief is the cruelest teacher,
the tug of war unable to be beaten by either
one of you.
It drowned you in sorrow, made you feel as if there was no
point in tomorrow
it showed you true love and what happens when it gets
ripped apart,
you carry its talons carefully against your heart.

Grief is the cruelest teacher,
but the most loyal friend
a companion that wouldn't leave you towards the end
it opened itself up to you,
let you swim in the waters it carried in its chest
waiting for you to feel at ease in the unrest
you are never alone when you are with grief
its cautious voice carries beside you like a pocket
handkerchief.

Grief reminds us that we are alive,
even though it hurts to survive
as it walks beside us.
The volume of it's cries will soften,
and you will think of it often,
your heart will begin to ease, your mind once again start to
imagine,
your clouded days will brighten and you will see that,
Grief is a simply teacher and trusted companion.

I lay
face down in the lake
I see your face
I come up for air
I see that you are not there
I stare upon the water
my gaze does not falter

I wonder what it would take
for you to notice
our feelings were not fake

We believed our meeting was fate
or perhaps due to a wandering gaze
either way, I was led to you,
how naive to think that
it would not hurt once we were through.

When you think of beauty and of grace
I know that it is for her you carve the space
for I will always be second place
to the girl who keeps your heart locked in good faith
it dulls my eyes to see
that there is not a space for me
to be entangled in a new memory.

My girlfriend firmly told me *'you have to stop falling for artists, for when they break your heart they will turn it into works of art.'*

Looking upon her as the words fell from her lips, I asked,

'Why should they be the only ones to heal,
is my heart not valid enough to feel pain so real?
I hold them close to my chest and speak only the best,
they turn my life into a melody, I turn them into everlasting poetry.'

You gave all your love away
to boys who could not change
you bled yourself dry
your eyes continued to cry
for the ones who did not even know the true meaning of
your name.

You dig your loved ones grave
every time you give in to yourself
and say
you are not enough
and you have no reason to stay.

DEEP SEA

Wading in the depths of you,
a place so stable my feet could never reach.
Gentle like snow, I was trying to let you know,
screaming love letters from my lungs,
I beseech you to use your tongue
to share what only your heart grew to know.

Your favourite type of morning
is one that you cannot explain.
It is merely a feeling,
a look upon your face,
the first coffee that you taste,
the way you say my name.
Your favourite morning
is one of simplicity
burning with the electricity
of not knowing what is in store
once you step out of your front door.

A FOOLS ERRAND:

Holding out for you.

My skin is soft,
but it can turn to salt.
Watch how I change
as you bring this love to a halt.

WAX AND WANE

You wanted the moon
I tried to give her to you
when I was full
when I was cold
you only wanted me as a crescent
bent into shape, curved to suit.
I pulled the tides close
showed you the beauty of the night
yet you eclipsed the light
that was meant for you.
You asked for the moon
when I gave myself to you
your eyes were looking upon the horizon
you couldn't see what had been found
waiting for the sun to come back around.

It was your world, baby, I just lived in it.
Now I'm rebuilding a new life,
not teetering on the edge of a knife
one where I don't have to be delicate.

Sweetened by your affection,
your lingering impression,
may I make a confession?
I am at an intersection of apprehension
whether you are the exception
or I am blinded by infatuation.

IN HIDING

I am able to suppress
the things I do not wish to undress
just as florals wilt in the fall
I too grow down and become small
I do not wish to live them over and over
even the mightiest struggle to stand tall.
Memories are faced with a cold shoulder
my mind rests
when the unwelcome house guests
linger quietly in the corner.
Peace at last,
I hope it will hold steadfast.

Silences between lovers
shouts louder
than any raised voice could.

Sunshine on your face
my arms around your waist
Summer tastes like pineapple and oranges,
frozen margaritas,
ice sliding down your throat.
You have dusted off the coat
of loneliness
gave up the solitary fight,
gave in to the feeling of someone new
something that you knew
would help bring you back to life.

BLOOD SUCKER

You're buzzing around my head
falling in and out of my bed
I can't stand the sounds of you.
The high pitch rises
I can never eradicate the whine
how you seem to grow three sizes
playing tricks on my mind.
What will it take
to remove you from my life
so I can finally rest in silence without trife.

Stars fell to the sea
sucking on my cheeks
looking up towards the moon
waiting for the fragility of youth
to wash out of my body.

MERINO

Hold me close and hold me warm
your laughter the port in this storm
I can see you smile
I can feel your love
even when you are far from reach
you still preach
gentle kindness.

You are able to teach
something I cannot,
a presence that encapsulates your essence
holds those around you who have endured
more than their hearts can hold.
I've never needed to be reassured
knowing that you've always got me
and I will have you
until we embrace again.

You wanted something I could never give you
I wanted the piece of me that he took away
while I fought with myself to stay.
It ate me from the inside out,
my breath grew shallow,
my eyes sank hollow.
Christmas came and New Years went
my emotions well spent,
by January I didn't recognise who I was,
my mind an endless fog.
I said goodbye, I hardly cried
& kept searching for the piece he took away.

I catch between my teeth
the missing piece
of the daydream that holds onto you.

He was quiet and he was kind
he would dance under moonlight
he was tall and he would flatter
he made you feel like you really did matter.
His eyes were wide & his feet planted on the ground
he was the one that let you down.

We said goodbye
for the last time
& I did not cry
for all the tears had fallen out of me
the last time we tried.

SABOTAGE

I sabotage myself
to let you shine
I give my heart away
I really thought I had learnt this time
you're not the one that got away
you are the one that won't stay.

My heart breaks for you
when you give yourself over to
those who do not care
who tentatively hold your heart,
you continue to see the good
while they weren't in it from the start.

I hide the framed pictures of you
for I don't want anyone to know
how deep my love for you
really goes.

MELT

Rub my head, ease the knot in my shoulder
as the days grow colder,
I do not think that my weary bones can soldier
on as they used to
before they knew what it was like to be held by you.

IN THE END

It seems that I will be known only as your friend
never again the one that you love
or the one that you held so high above
the others that come after.
My friend,
you will be the one that I treasure
until the very end.

My head pounds
with the sound
of your fingertips as they brush against my ribcage
slowly they split
sharing the secrets my lips were too afraid to say.

ON FIRE FOR YOU

eyes burn
souls yearn
fate has taken a turn
during your solar return.

THE WEIGHT

I skate around the park
once or twice in the dark, trying to ease the feeling of a
broken heart -
One that is not mine,
but a burden that I carry quietly inside.

This feeling will ease with time
unless you ignore the warning signs -
Maybe not tonight or tomorrow,
but soon, one day
the truth of your heart you'll follow.

BEACH, BABY

The song plays on repeat
a record crackles in the dark
I can hear his words in my sleep.
It's been like this for weeks,
staring out at the sea,
holding on and waiting to breathe
out the deceit that won't set me free,
praying I don't become obsolete.

SUGAR RUSH

Is it cruel of me to expect too much
from the one who gives me a sugar rush?
Keep quiet, don't scare off
a little Spring crush.
You don't know how it will bloom,
if it does not have the room
to grow.

Shooting arrows through my own heart
just trying to feel something in the dark.

BETTY

You gave me a ring for luck
to help when my life became unstuck
it would be a reminder
to only ever decipher
kind words from a stranger
& when to step into my power.
You bought yourself one just the same, for you are my twin
flame.

Treat yourself with kindness,
find yourself in lightness
darkness won't last forever
you'll always have me to hold your hand, even in the
stormiest of weather.

Nettles that sting
have replaced petals
upon my bedside table.
The phone does not ring
as it once used to
there is a fable that runs through my mind
keeping me in place
parting the space
that does not belong to you anymore.

SILENT KILLER

Bite the hand that feeds
you let it fester before it bleeds
echos whisper *'we could have saved her.'*
You scream to the sky
rain falling upon your face *'why why why'*
it will never absolve
the way you turned a blind eye.

My hands are numb
my heart is too,
the one to mend them
will it be you?

If the music wasn't so loud
I would've asked if it was okay
to kiss you on the mouth.

You, Her
what transpired before,
I am not here to shove my foot through the door
that was only meant for the two of you.
I am here to renew,
hoping that you can see through
the apprehension that has taken residence in my body
while I am learning us,
for I will not be a carbon copy
of the one that hurt you.

I tried to fill the hollow of your neck
with the words that you deserved to hear
ones I could not take back,
I whispered them while you slept
so that your body would not forget
how treasured you really are.

A pulsing vein feels the same as your name
when it falls from my mouth
as I try to explain
this will be different
you are not to blame
for the way I exclaim
how love has caused me such pain.

Kissing apologies into my neck
to help me see you were true,
never to forget
how right I was to carve the space for you.

You told me my eyes were pretty
the way they changed from blue to grey.
You should see how they shine
when I look at you in the dark of night
& glow of the day.

A hum in your throat
words at your fingertips,
hands, a moment on my hips
you, a lifetime upon my lips.

I am finding it hard
always being a sacrifice for my art
I do not know how much my heart can take
when I continue to give it away.
When will I learn
that I do not need to yearn
for a love that makes me burn
both inside and out.

Birds of a feather
like hell is to leather
we fit very nicely together.

Lips stained persimmon
hair kissed by marigold
one was shy, one was bold
this was a story nobody could have foretold
how will it unfold?
When one was tightly controlled
the other was unable to be consoled.

MANIPULATION

It is the worst kind of 'love'
you want someone to have and to hold
a little doll
somebody you can control
Qui suis-je? Je ne sais pas.
Does it make you happy
that I am barely hanging on?
Are *you* going to save *me?*
Erreur. J'en ai fini avec ça.
I was in mourning
I let my guard down
you should be the one to come with a danger warning.
Au revoir, bon débarras.

You took my troubles and called them by name
speaking them out loud, helps dull the pain
easing the burden upon my brain.
No longer do I strain
to keep them hidden within my chest,
you are always helping me see the best,
helping me to invest in something brighter that makes
sense.

Hold your head up high
the only pedestal that you fall from
is the one they built in their own sky.

You say you're not at your best
because you haven't had rest all week,
you don't need to be at your peak
for I will always treasure the words you speak.

You have a sweet way of drawing words out of me
falling like molasses, untethered they seem to be.
Uncensored
my mouth moves faster than my brain
it doesn't refrain from what it cannot explain
spilling endlessly out towards this new terrain
you are the guide that keeps me from flying blind
how lucky I am to have you on my side.

BOY SCOUT

Boy scout,
didn't they teach you what to do when the fire goes out?
You can't leave the kindling in the rain
even though picking it up is a real pain,
care you mustn't feign.

Didn't you get your merit badge?

You have to relight it soon
otherwise you will face the wilderness alone
without the warmth beside you.
Boy scout, try to see this one through.

DROWNING

Treading water is easy when you haven't been at it long
murky water and algae,
let's make a bet
are you going to get your hair wet?
Breathing deep
I sink underwater
here you can't touch the bottom
you don't know how far it goes.
What would happen if I let myself fall
stopped my legs from kicking, arms resting at my sides
would I discover something down below?
A small sacrifice to see what lurks beneath our feet.
Treading water is easy,
when your soul isn't weighing heavy.

Wind howls
my dog growls
I'm running out of vowels
to help me explain what I long to say
can I have a consonant
or perhaps something constant
to help me feel a certain type of way?

It can be debilitating
living in a stream of conscious waiting
for someone to be reciprocating
the feelings that they were having trouble translating
maybe they will continue hibernating
until the silence becomes isolating.

Bells toll at the cathedral. Something called to me, the architecture maybe, I wasn't looking for God, I was looking for silence. People much older than me sat, backs poised in pews, their mouths moving silently in unison. Dressed all in black, they weren't here for a funeral, hands clasped together they braced as if they were withstanding harsh weather.

I watched as a man raised his hands to the steeple, he bowed his head and called out to his people, *'here you have found a home, here you may atone, the sins of others are not the sins of yours.'*

I went looking for silence, something crushing to drown out the noise of my own head, I felt like I was suffocating. Would I ever find peace? Not in this place.
The bells toll at the cathedral, ravens perch upon the roof, this is an omen unspoken.

LEAGUE

I must have emotional fatigue
always chasing after those I think aren't in my league
ones that shine brighter than I ever could
maybe I've lost sight of who I am
projecting a falsehood
upon suitors
that could only tutor me
in the art of breaking myself in two.

They tell me I deserve better than to fall for someone who changes as quickly as Melbourne weather.

However, my mind continues to tell me that I know better.

Maybe my heart works better under pressure
not knowing if it will be in pain or pleasure -
if I will be someone's trash or treasure.

All we are is skin and bone
wandering this earth
until we find a place we can rest
where we unleash our best
somewhere our minds can roam
a place we can call home.

It's a shame to think that I was close to taking your name
but there was a fire that you could not tame
that resided in my own flame
one that you will never be able to claim.

HUSH HUSH

Delicate touch,
lovers rush,
make my cheeks flush,
you've turned my brain to mush
with this silly little crush.

Your jealousy of him
is only because
he gave me things you could not.
Do not poison something good
with your lack of adulthood.

LOVE LETTER TO MY FRIENDS

There is a magnetism to you
that I have not found in any other
knowing what I'm about to say before I have the chance to
utter
the love that runs from my soul
to
yours.

IT'S 3AM AGAIN

Spent time becoming acquainted with my bathroom floor.

For it was the only place for me to pour out the emotions
that nowhere else could hold. I held my body close, afraid
to keep it open and exposed.
I've woken up here more times than I can count, sleep
carrying me from warm covers and towards cold tiles.
Goosebumps upon my skin, my hands frozen red, my lips
a shade of blue, they never said that healing would be easy
but I didn't know each day I would be living in a state of
deja-vu.
Will the feeling ever pass or will I remain in a silent
suffocators grip, my life at an impasse one I know I can't
conquer on my own.

A HEART IN TOKYO

two frayed friendship bracelets and 6,821kms between us
but I hope you know that I love you, always.

8 HOUR FACETIME

Thank you for letting me call you until 2am because I
didn't understand my own mind.
You're one of a kind, my best friend, my beginning and my
end.

Holding your friends hands in public is normal
watching their heart ache over a coffee is not.

Please friend, do not feel as if this has to be formal
while you're at my table cry if you wish, laugh loudly if
you desire
my heart is always open. Willing and able.

TWO SCOOPS

We walked along Brunswick Street,
our bellies full but still wanting to taste something sweet.
You sat outside in the pouring rain eating ice-cream with
me,
it was 9 degrees
you said that we didn't have to leave, I watched as
raindrops fell down your sleeve.
Patiently you listened as I poured my life out, sage advice
fell from your mouth.
my soul cannot hold the amount of affection I wish to
bestow
times like this, mean more to me than you'll ever know.

THE TWO YEAR WAIT

The first kiss; the first hug,
the first time you ask what have you been up to?
Only to be met with a laugh and a shrug
'Nothing, what is there to do?'
The first tears that fall from finally being able to see you
we all wanted to take time away
but didn't want to be separated
we spent the days inside as skies turned grey
we waited, we let our emotions stray.
Months of being deflated, suddenly erased
as I see your face, elated.

'I've missed you, what have you been up to?'
'That can wait, we have so much to do.'

Ghosts of the past
will haunt you until you turn on the light
or till their last
dying breath.

LITTLE LOVE,
BIG FEELINGS

Your charm keeps me hanging off of your arm,
your voice in the morning is my soundtrack of choice,
the comforting smell of the one you are getting to know
well,
your sneakers strewn across the floor and your t-shirt
hanging on my door,
your energy calm, the soothing balm, how easily you
disarm,
your mind chaotic, you find me to be the antibiotic
little moonbeam, you are no longer just a daydream
it is heaven sent, the time we have, spent forgetting the rest
of the world exists, at least for a moment.

We're undefined and slowly I begin to lose my mind,
will I continue to wander blind while you treat me unkind?
I remain confined to feelings which make me inclined
to spellbind my feelings within one I cannot leave behind.

Don't waste your time
on those who would turn on a dime.
For your radiance and shine
is worth more than any heartbreak
or inspirational comment of mine.

The most beautiful I've ever seen you -
you were sitting on the edge of a bathtub
eyes half closed,
toothbrush hanging from your mouth
illuminated by the light from your phone
so blissfully unaware, you did not care
I looked upon you and the glimpse of your tattoo
wishing that you knew
à quel point je suis ravi de toi.

SAD/LIFE

I feel endlessly sad
For a life that I've yet to have.
My heart aches for the memories that are to come, the
places I will one day roam.
My chest is heavy with expectations of myself, ones that
render me useless most days.

Life is a precious, beautiful and ever changing thing - one
that we cannot control or hope to understand.
Knowing that there is so much to experience, a series of
moments that are better left unplanned.

I long for the future, I pine for the past, I am blind to what
is happening in front of me.

My hope is to outlast the thoughts in my head, welcome
each day with kindness and to know that life will be
waiting with arms open spread.

I speak about you to everyone as yours is the only name
stuck under my tongue

You kissed me at the river, your hair sopping wet
so gentle it made my mind forget that my day had been a
mess.
You kissed my neck underneath the trees
the very weight of it made me weak in the knees.
I would drive in endless silence with you
but that would be impossible between us two.
You are a comfort
I am at a loss.

MARCUS

My sweet golden, brown-eyed boy
he had no want for anything other than love or a soft toy
He would beam like the sun every time he would run
toward someone he loved
My darling, my little love, one who I cannot let go of.
I search for him everywhere I go
I hope and pray that an endless love is one he will always
know,
even if he is far away.

Rain falls
sinking into the yellowing grass
quenching an endless dehydration
flies buzz in the window sill
I read the words my friends have written, their loving
experiences carefully curated inside of soft cover books
the air is damp and my clothes are warm, my body heavy
with gratitude and my eyes filled with proud tears
my golden girl sleeps beside me on the floor, front paws
padding against the carpet, racing dreams
freshly brewed coffee awaits me at the table
cat curled upon my lap.
If it was all to end, I wouldn't shed a tear
for home is here and now.

FEEL IT ALL

I have never been able to contain all that is within, like a
teacup that overflows, emotions used to spill from my tiny
body, shaking as I grew, they now fall out of this bigger
one too.

Old couples in love pull at my heartstrings, young people
figuring it out makes me hopeful.
I'm enraged by injustices that I cannot solve, passion
barrels out of me as I try to make things a little better than
before.
Tears fall in the darkness of the cinema, enraptured by the
way a hand brushes against a shoulder, both on screen and
off.

It is both a blessing and a curse to be able to feel
everything
all at once,

an overwhelming sensory experience one that cannot be
explained, unless you too feel with every part of your
being.

Hold onto the feeling, run into the darkness with it, it might
overwhelm, but it's something that is going to save you.

Sighs, my thighs,
wishes and wants,
too much
yet I'm still not enough.

You kiss me in the kitchen
let the fridge light the secrets you spill, the room washing
white.
You come alive at night
your eyes wide and your voice quiet
the moon hangs low and you dance with me slow,
silently slinking toward your room
one breath, shared by two.

EMOTIONAL VAMPIRE

A bride and a groom
surrounded by love
how sweet it is to consume
all the feelings in the room.
I take what I can carry
I expel it back out
my teeth in the neck of your worry
replacing it with the feeling
of something anew.

THE HOLLOWS

My thoughts turn to you in the deepest parts of my sleep
they turn to you in the hollows of my dream.

Do not go where darkness follows for you will sink into
your chest
where light used to rest
that little cavern in your chest will not feel deep unrest
forever -
You will find the change that you seek, the wishes and
heartfelt needs,
they will come to you in time, you will see.

Your ocean is wide and vast
the hollows of your life are tiny drops in the sea,
sadness will not last, your grief will not swallow you
whole,
sit with your feelings & search your soul
for the hollows are gentle reminders
that you, sweet darling, still have so far to go.